A Tale in Time

A Tale in Tin

The Necklace Chrc

Philip and Chelsea Books

Willow George

1

A Tale in Time

Author: Willow George

Published: 25/02/2020

ISBN: 978-0-244-86615-0

A Tale in Time

Contents

A Tale in Time

The Thieves of Rose Road

Chapter 1: The Rivets

Rose Road was a road, yes, but an ugly road at that. The houses were terraced, each with once grand steps leading up to their doors, but they were now shabby, the gutter was filled with rubbish and the cars that passed through were mere traffic and never stopped to let any of the passengers out. No one who lived on Rose Road was rich enough to take a taxi anywhere, everyone was poor and the houses were divided into flats.

During World War Two, life had been extreme and many of the men of Rose Road had died. Few returned. But Rose Road was as busy as ever and London was a prosperous place. The widowed women set to work, most remarried, and the children played on the front steps if they were not wanted.

Now it happened that one family, called the Rivets, had lived on Rose Road for more then fifty years. Mrs Rivet was a lucky woman and her husband returned, but lamed, and unable to do anything but be a burden, so most of the other women pitied Mrs Rivet.

The Rivets had four children: two girls and two boys. The eldest was eighteen-year-old Mack, who had been apprenticed to a blacksmith and now was a partner in the business and sent his money home.

Fifteen-year-old twins Polly and John were both doing their duties; John stayed at home half the week to tend to the vegetable garden and repair the falling-down house (the Rivets were one of the few families to own an entire house), but the other half of the week he worked at the markets, moving crates of vegetables and fruit. Polly worked as a seamstress for a dressmaker, and so she got lots of left over material and therefore made the family clothes.

The last child was twelve-year-old Margaret; she was better known as May. The reason for this nickname was that she had been born in a fresh, summery May twelve years ago, and the month of May had always brought them luck. They had tried Meg as a nickname a few times but May had stuck, and Mr Rivet returned from the war, calling for "Mack, Polly, John and Meg," and had been greeted by three children. "Where is Meg?" he had asked his wife. "Ah! May!" she had replied.

Mrs Rivet was a stout plump lady, she was a lovely cook and loved babies, so she babysat children often. May, too young to work, had been obliged to help her mother about the house, and today was her day off, Sunday, and she sat on the steps with an expression of relief.

May Rivet was little with a timid friendly face, brown hair and welcoming, ready blue eyes. She was strong and hard-working despite her size, and when she had helped a woman collect her missing puppies, a few years ago in the midst of war, despite her mother's forbade, she had been rewarded with a choice of a puppy and chose Jo.

Jo was two-years old, a terrier-cross, short haired, bright, white, black and brown, resembling a smooth-haired Fox Terrier, and ever-loyal to May. Jo was little and hadn't been hard to feed, and now followed May around eagerly as she did her daily tasks.

Now, May put her arms around Jo and looked out on the busy street.

A Tale in Time

Unlike most siblings, the four got on unusually well, and the others found the friendship between dog and child touching, so they all used their wages to make Jo a grand dog. Polly used stout leather to make a collar and then a lead with a soft handle, Mack welded some metal bowls for her and John brought a nice dog-basket.

The street was dirty and busy, few people looked twice at May and Jo, but Mack, returning for a week's holiday, walked up the gutter. For a moment neither recognised the other; Mack had grown very tall, above six feet, and his light brown hair had darkened to a sooty coal-black, and May was thinner, a little taller, and besides, she held a dog in her arms; Mack had been away for two years and had not yet met Jo, and assumed a little girl was sitting on his mother's steps.

A Tale in Time

"Shoo!" he said imperiously. May
recognised him and rose, giving a slight cry,
"Mack!" then he knew her as his sister.
"Margaret!" "Mother will be so glad," she said
warmly and she led the way inside. Everyone
was there; Polly sat stitching, Mrs Rivet was in
the kitchen washing a barrel of sheets, Mr
Rivet sat in his armchair scribbling away at a
book he hoped to publish as 'A Journal of
Battle Experience' and John was peeling
potatoes fresh from the garden with a weary
attitude.

"Look!" said May excitedly. "It is Mack!"
The family greeted him, he sat down and
looked about himself, and said laughing, "Polly,
you are rather the young lady!" "So I am," she
retorted sharply. Mack glanced to his other
sister curiously. She, as if out of place, sat by
the fire, her arms full of Jo and her face warily

alert.

Chapter 2: A Gift

May was bored and so she decided to take Jo to the recreational ground, which was twenty minutes' walk away. She set off quietly and no one missed her.

At the gate of the park was a dirty beggar child and she said in a hoarse voice, "Oh, oh miss, could I just pat your dog?" May crouched down, and said warmly but shortly, "Yes, of course!" The child stroked Jo with a look of love. "Here, if you want you can come and walk her with me in the park. She chases sticks," said May. "Yes," said the child blindly and they walked on through the gate.

"What's your name?" began May in a friendly tone as the child threw sticks into the grass for the little terrier. "Statty," she heard the mumble. "Statty what?" "Well, my brother called me Statty," burst out the child, "but my name is really Josephine O'Connor." "Irish?" said May quickly, for her grandmother had been Irish and talked of the countryside in a reverent tone. "Yes," said Josephine, "and don't I wish I was back there, 'stead of here where you call *this* a park!" and she gazed scornfully about the little patch of grass. As if remembering her manners, she said, "Well, who are you?" "Margaret Rivet," said May. "And my dog's Jo." "Jo!" said Josephine. "Sounds like my name!" "It does," replied May shortly.

After several laps of the park, May decided to go home. "Are you homeless?" she said. "No. My brother is at work and then he takes us to our aunt's for the night. But our aunt is a demon and I *hate* her. So I'm outdoors." May had Jo on the lead and the child said goodbye.

A Tale in Time

Just before May left, Josephine ran up, and shouted, "*Wait!*" "What is it?" said May. "You've been so kind — I got a gift," said the child as if uncomfortable, and she held out a grubby coil of metal. "Why, thank you," said May, whose instinct told her not to argue and press the worthless chain back on her little friend, but to accept it and be grateful.

She walked back a roundabout way to her home, stroking the metal. On a impulse she ran into a goldsmiths, and said, "Hello sir! Will you look at something of mine and tell me what it is?" "Well, have you money?" said the greedy goldsmith. "No," sighed May, who was used to doing odd jobs if she wanted something but didn't have money, "but I'll sweep your floor if you give me a broom." "You do that," he replied, so she did, and as she worked industriously, panting and trying to catch her breath, he cleaned the chain and then carefully looked at it under a bright light. As he handed it back, he simply said, "Well, you've got money now."

This strange choice of words echoed in May's mind as she walked with Jo, gazing at the chain. It was evidently a necklace, made of gold with a silver clasp, and worth lots. May's first impulse was to rush back to Josephine O'Connor and tell her she'd made a mistake, and she could not accept it, but then she shook her head, sighed and went on, stroking the chain. She eventually put it on and ran up the steps of her house.

"Oh May! May!" Polly was crying. "Oh May, John has taken ill and we have no money to get a doctor!" May thought of her necklace. Sorry as she was to part with it, she was as kind as she was friendly, and the years of war, danger, death, sorrow and hunger had made her used to sacrifices. "Wait," she said, and depositing an outraged Jo on the stairs, she raced out again. "Where is Margaret, Polly?" said Mrs Rivet from the kitchen door where she soaked rags to soothe her son's forehead. "She came in and she has gone out again," said Polly, pale with anxiety.

May ran to the goldsmith that she had gone to only an hour ago, and threw herself in the door. But it was a different person. "Oh, take my necklace," she said with a little impatience. The elderly man took it, shook his head and said in a knowledgeable way, "It's not worth anything, little girl. But if you need money, you may as well as not go to the tearoom opposite and say to the manager you'll be a waitress this afternoon."

So May did so, and worked so hard that

she served double customers and got double money, though every minute cost her dear and it was a good two hours of exhaustion. Then she summoned the doctor. When John was being treated, she sat on the stairs holding an indignant Jo to her and feeling weary. But even so, there was no rest, she had to go and do plenty of sewing and fine embroidery that made her feel her so exhausted that she went to bed early without her dinner and she slept long and hard.

Chapter 3: The Amber

One kindness must rebound and Josephine O'Connor gifted the necklace to May, then May needed to sell it against her wishes and yet didn't have to and gained her desire in a different way.

The next day, May was feeling in a better spirit and worked so very hard! Polly was working and Mack did the garden, so May worked at some stitchery, then she helped Mrs Rivet at some washing. Then Mr Rivet gave her a spelling lesson, while she did knitting. Then she had to be a nurse to the poorly John. It was afternoon by the time she was not wanted, and she took Jo and simply ran down the alleys, dodging cars and people alike with her eyes full of a haunted weariness.

Suddenly she fell and she gave a cry. Jo

scampered into the road and May shrieked. A high voice called, "Jo! Jo!" and glancing about, she saw Jo in the arms of Josephine O'Connor! She picked up the little paper package she had slipped on and then ran eagerly across the road to Josephine. "Thank you so," she said. "Ah, that's okay," said Josephine nonchalantly. "Can't have Jo get lost, can we?" "No. See, Josephine, I still have your necklace safe," and May produced it eagerly. "Ah, it looks so clean!" said Josephine. She was then called by an old lady-voice and had to rush into a grubby house and away.

"Well, Jo!" said May as she walked back. "I think I'd better see what I slipped on." She carefully opened the package. It was an amber. "An amber, Jo!" she whispered in amazement. Then, with a sudden thought, she chained the amber onto the necklace.

A Tale in Time

It suddenly vibrated and gave a queer shake. Then May was in a dark hole, Jo beside her whining, and the necklace spoke! "You have united me with my other part and deserve the noble thanks of immortality. You, Lady May, are now in the ownership of the magical wishing necklace — you may go anywhere you desire, and have anything you wish. You are a rich child." "Me!" said May, never disbelieving for a moment, but feeling terribly lucky.

"What is your first wish?" said the necklace. "For Jo to talk," said May. "Granted," the necklace replied, "anything else?" "I wish to adventure on myself, but I want my family to have as much money and things that they could desire," said May. Then she said, "Now I want to go to the top of the highest mountain!" and then she was!

A Tale in Time

"What a view," she said to Jo with a tiny gasp. Holding the necklace tenderly, she gazed out across the top of the Himalayas. She was on Mount Everest. "Now I fall silent," said the necklace calmly. "But if you want anything from me, simply turn the amber three times and wish."

May did up the necklace on her neck and then sat down. "I wish for a breakfast of beef sandwiches," she said. "What do you want, Jo?" "Chicken bones," said Jo in a perfectly fluent way that shocked and delighted May beyond all.

During the breakfast, May found out about Jo's personality, Jo was strong and cheeky and humorous, a perfect contrast to May's own character and so in this way, they got on *perfectly.*

Chapter 4: The Hikers

But this peace was not to last, oh no! May wished for warm, fine clothes, and was granted them. She chose a blue velvet dress, sky-blue, and thick and warm. She ate a Mars chocolate bar, which was absolute heaven to her, and Jo had a fine piece of goose breast which she declared was "absolutely *stunning.*"

But May never noticed the mountain-hikers behind her, and when they heard of her wondrous necklace they both made up their mind to steal it.

Rushing forward, one held Jo tightly whilst the other ripped the necklace off her neck, and then they stood still foolishly, for they did not know how to activate it!

May was a timid child, used to doing things without a reason why, used to sacrifices and hardship, and used to working hard. With the find of her splendid necklace, however, her character changed, and without knowing it herself, she was more bold and eager then before.

With a terrific strength, she tore herself out of her captor's grasp, and then she rolled on her side dangerously toward the peak-edge, but righted herself in time and flung herself on the man holding Jo.

She wrenched her dog free, and Jo said quickly, "Now then, thieves, how shall you get away?" with a recklessness that May admired instantly.

"With your — sorry, *our* — necklace," they replied triumphantly.

Here May found her dragon temper she never knew existed, she saw Josephine O'Connor's big warm eyes as she gifted the necklace, and heard her shout "Jo!" as May fell over on the magic amber, and an outrage filled her.

She gave a tremendous shout, "I think *not!"* and launched herself forward at the man who had snatched Jo (Eric Barterhat), knocking him straight off the peak. "NOOO!" he cried as he tumbled onto a stony ledge, in terrible agony.

The other man watched her nervously, she watched him with a terrible look of loathing, and wished she could push him too. But her necklace — oh her precious necklace! It was in his hands, and if she pushed him, the amber might swing, he might vanish, and then where would she be?

Jo, however, was pluckier then her; she charged forward and nipped the man on the back of his leg, so he fell forward. Then she growled into his face and he shrieked girlishly,

as May tore the necklace from him.

Then, holding onto Jo, they vanished away

— but the thief (Ritchie Lodge), with no

thought of his poor comrade groaning pitifully,

held onto Jo's leg and went with them.

(What became of Eric Barterhat is

unknown, but it is assumed he died, for no one

ever heard of him again.)

Chapter 5: "You say I mustn't,"

May leapt across Rose Road. In her despair she realised she had brought herself home for help.

Seeing Polly cleaning the steps with a scrubbing-brush, she shouted, "Help!" and made her look up.

"Margaret Rivet!" said Polly, shooing Ritchie Lodge away imperiously. May grabbed hold of her sister in relief.

"Oh Polly, it has been an adventure! You'd never know what has happened to me. That man there — oh!" For the man had a fighting, biting Jo under his arm!

"JO!" shouted May, tearing after her dog in a desperate manner.

But it was no use. Mr Lodge disappeared down an alleyway and although May raced after him wildly, he vanished. And so did Jo.

A Tale in Time

Polly had come after her. Fond of her quaint sister May, she was sad to see Jo go.

She led May back consolingly, but May wasn't to be comforted. She raged, mourned and wept in the same instant. Then she remembered her necklace.

She grasped hold of her chain and bent down, ignoring Polly's and now Mrs Rivet's curious glances, she started talking to it.

"Oh Amber, Amber, the most dreadful thing has happened. My poor dog Jo has been stolen! I must have her back. I must. Please bring her to me."

She said this loudly, with an utmost faith in the charm that had magic, that had once spoken to her, that had reassured her that her every need was to be satisfied.

And the amber, although it had previously said it was going to be silent forevermore, listened to her plea, felt deeply sympathetic as

it remembered being split from its other half,

the

golden chain, and spoke.

"I will help you child! But you must be

brave and have a great strength of mind.

There is nothing you cannot do if I help you,

which I will."

This was obviously calming to poor May,

who said, "Now what?" "Go down to Josephine

O'Connor's house," it commanded her.

She made to leave. But Mrs Rivet quickly

snatched her arm. "We will have another dog

for you, Margaret darling, but you mustn't go

just now, after you have been so vacant; such

wondrous riches have happened to us and it

seems *you* have a tale to tell too!"

May was a different child. In fact she was

no longer the shy helpful girl, the youngest of

the Rivet children, who had a little rogue

terrier, Jo. Because of this, she said shortly,

"Mother, there is no other option. Poor dear Jo

is lost. I shall have no other dog. Your riches

and my absence are due to a bit of luck and a

gift; this, my amber necklace. It talks to me, it

helps me. It gives me what I desire. And I

desire Jo. And I shall have her." And with this,

she marched off.

"Polly, whatever is the matter with May?"

said Mrs Rivet, watching the small purposeful

figure march off. "I don't know Mother. It *is*

strange; we may only take her word,"

answered Polly. But her thoughts were far

away, as were Mrs Rivet's; they both were

thinking about May.

May had a tremendous determination; she

marched off with the amber guiding her.

She came across, much to her

exasperation, her brother John. "John!" she
exclaimed. "May!" he replied. "Whatever are
you doing *here*?" "Searching for Jo. She has
been stolen," said May irritably. "Ah, poor
doggy. Now sis, come on. No point looking for
her; I'd have seen her," said John. But the
amber was urging her to go on; May felt it.

"No, no, *no*!" she insisted. "You don't
understand what has happened to me, John,
all sorts have, magic and stuff. Anyway, I'm
the reason why we're rich. So I am *going* to
find Jo."

"No, no, dear, we'll get you another," said
John crossly. "You say I mustn't, but I will!"
said May fiercely. And she walked off.

Chapter 6: Hard Times for Jo

Jo was having a hard time of it. Bundled under Mr Lodge's arm, she had given up struggling and lay limply, thinking out a strategy to escape.

She had no fear that May would rescue her, however she was a proud little terrier and didn't want to be rescued unless the situation was extreme. She knew perfectly well how to look after herself.

"Ha, I've shut your gob, haven't I?" said Mr Lodge triumphantly. Unlike her frank mistress, Jo was secretive and sly; however, at a prod from her captor, she answered in a somewhat sulky tone.

"No. Terriers of my sort *don't* give up," she informed him.

"Oh ho! Is that so? Well, I think you will

soon," laughed Mr Lodge in a terrible voice,

and for the first time, Jo began to feel petrified.

"May will come and rescue me with the

necklace. You failed to get that, didn't you?"

she said bravely.

"Hmm, I did. But I will soon have it," was

the mysterious answer, and both fell silent.

Jo was brought into a house, and shoved

into a cellar. The door was locked and she was

left in darkness.

She prowled around, searching and sniffing.

She found some rather old water, and avoided

drinking it. Then she saw a board, covering a

hole in the wall that led to another room.

Hearing footsteps on the stairwell, she

hurried back to the door, hoping to escape that

way. But it was opened very cautiously, and

she sighed and withdrew herself.

A Tale in Time

A woman walked in. She had an ugly, wrinkled face, and a broom in her hand. She raised the broom at Jo, and the dog backed away.

"Now dog, Ritchie told me you can speak," she said coldly.

"I can indeed, but whether I wish to speak to *you* or not remains unseen," said Jo a great deal more braver then she felt.

"Ha ha! An insolent arrogant dog we have here!" said the woman. She shut the door behind her and said sternly, "Now, who is your owner?"

Jo thought about it for a moment and then decided to tell the truth.

"Margaret Rivet," she said in a low tone. "And is she the owner of the necklace?" said the woman. "Yes," said Jo shortly. "Where does she live?"

A Tale in Time

"On Rose Road," said Jo. "Hmm, you have told me all I wish to know. There will be potato peelings for you later," said the woman and, hastened by a shout from Mr Lodge, she departed.

"Oh May, whatever have we got ourselves into?" said Jo desperately. Then she pattered across to the board.

She cautiously pulled it away at the bottom corners and then gnawed it with her teeth. She worked on it for some hours, then she pulled upwards, releasing the board totally.

At last she got into the other room and heard a faint wailing.

"Rats! Rats!" screamed the voice as she walked over.

It was a girl. She was at least fourteen, with curly black hair and big brown eyes. She

A Tale in Time

inspected Jo in a dim candlelight with relief, stopped screaming and said in a dignified tone, "Thank goodness you *aren't* a rat, or you'd have got a hot-wax bath."

Jo felt rustled at this cold greeting and said haughtily, "I am not a rat. I am a dog."

"I know that, Miss High and Mighty Talking Dog! Are you a prisoner too?" said the girl.

"Yes. I got in by the board interlinking our cellars," and Jo gestured with her nose.

"I am Ursula Night," began the girl, then she raised a hand. "Hush!" she exclaimed. "Do you hear that noise?"

Jo listened and heard a soft hooting. The girl gave a hoot back, and suddenly they were in the presence of a boy.

He was the same age as May, with grubby cheeks and curly brown hair. He didn't see Jo at first and crawled across the cellar silently

35

until he was next to Ursula.

"Hello there," he said, producing a small paper bag. "That's dinner, Ursula. Heard any rats?" he said this last with a cheeky smile.

"Oh, you wicked boy, no, of course not," said Ursula crossly. "Thank you for the dinner, Davy."

Then Davy saw Jo. "Who are you?" he whispered.

"I am Jo Rivet," said Jo proudly, "who are you?"

"Davy," he said, and as silently as he had arrived, he vanished.

"Who *is* that?" said Jo as Ursula inspected the contents of the paper bag.

"Davy. I don't know his surname. He is the nephew of the neighbours, and he managed to get through the cellars when he heard me shouting once. Ever since he gets me things to eat since Mrs Lodge doesn't," said Ursula,

giving a bit of chicken to Jo.

"Who are you?" said Jo once more. "Why,

Ursula Night, as I said. I used to be a maid to

Mrs Lodge. But then I eavesdropped on a chat

and she hit me and then imprisoned me," said

Ursula. "But Davy brought some blankets and

he brings food daily and candles if I need them.

Sometimes he sits and talks to me, but he

works every day so not often. Mr Lodge is

away on a mountain hike at the moment so

Mrs Lodge is particularly bad-tempered.

Anyway, who are *you*?"

"I am Jo Rivet. I am the dog of May Rivet.

She came across a magic amber necklace and

together we went away to a mountain peak.

But some hikers (one of which was Mr Ritchie

Lodge) tried to steal the necklace. Then May

and me got back to Rose Road, which is where

we live, but Mr Lodge managed to hold onto us and come with us. Then he stole me and ran off. But I've no doubt that May will rescue me," said Jo stoutly.

"May Rivet. Rose Road. Magic necklace. Hmm, what a tale!" said Ursula critically.

"True, though," said Jo. "Why didn't you escape through Davy's hole?" she added.

"Oh, because it is too small." "But do you think I could?" said Jo breathlessly. "Probably, but Davy's aunt might see you, I think she might even work with the Lodges," was Ursula's nonchalant reply.

Then, hearing footsteps on Ursula's flight of stairs, Jo turned and ran back into her own cellar.

Oh, would May rescue her from this dreadful imprisonment?

Chapter 7: Josephine's Aunt

May ran down the interlinking alleys and roads to Josephine's house. It was on a dirty narrow road, and she couldn't remember which house was Josephine's.

She stopped dead by a house, then, summoning courage, raised her hand to knock. As she did so, however, the door flew open and a tottering old lady departed. "Pray, who are you?" said the old lady with great dignity.

"Margaret," said May, somehow feeling cautious of the old woman and not wishing to say her name.

"I'm looking for Josephine O'Connor," she said. "But I'm not sure which house to go to; do you know?"

"I do indeed. That is *my* house. Josephine is my niece," said the woman, and she led May one house along, entered, and called for Josephine.

Josephine came. "May!" she said, her eyes brightening. "Where's Jo?" "Stolen," and May led Josephine away a little.

Then she repeated all her adventures from beginning to end. Josephine shook her head. "I wish I knew who Ritchie Lodge was. But I don't. Look, come back at dusk. My brother David comes back then, and he works as a newspaper boy, so *he* might know." "Okay," said May, sighing, but thinking it the best outcome possible.

And she walked away.

She could hardly bear to go back to her family. So many questions and so many pityingly glances she foresaw! How could she bear it without Jo?

So she wished herself some money and

had dinner in a café. Then she wandered around that particular area of London, returning as soon as dusk fell, and waiting outside Josephine's house patiently.

Soon enough she saw Josephine and a slightly older boy with her. The boy had curly brown hair and laughing eyes, but they were not laughing now, they were intensely curious.

The moment he saw May he said instantly "Are you the girl who's lost her doggy?" "I am," said May steadily, although her eyes grew moist with despair for her Jo.

"What's your name?" said the boy simply, leaning against the wall of his house, Josephine copying him. May stood alertly upright. "May Rivet," she said.

"*Oh!*" said the boy. "We'll need to get acquainted, we will, (*my* name's Davy), 'cos I know where Jo is, but you'll have come back..." he paused. "WHAT'S THAT?!" came the yell from somewhere. The two girls turned away.

Seeing nothing, May rotated her head to ask Davy where Jo was.

But Davy wasn't there!

Chapter 8: Davy, Jo and Ursula

"Well, we're a sorry sight," grinned the boy wryly. He sat struggling to untie the ropes that held his hands and feet together. He had curly brown hair and was tall but thin. His last memory was of a bag coming over his head with a rock inside it, that had then knocked him out.

His companions were restrained too; Jo was in a cage much too small for her and Ursula was tied like Davy.

They were in the back of a car, softly roaring down the quiet streets.

But where?

"It's rotten shame," huffed Ursula, kicking her feet madly in a hopeless attempt to free herself. "It should be illegal, it should!"

"Bingo!" said Davy, ignoring Ursula as he

freed a hand. Wriggling about, he freed his other hand and then his feet.

He crawled across the seating and started to untie Ursula, and then let Jo out of the cage. Jo sprang out and lay flexing every limb she had for joy.

"I was a-going to tell your mistress how to get to you," said Davy to Jo, "but then Aunt distracted me."

"Oh, does she work with them too?" said Ursula in interest. "I thought she did, but I didn't know." "She does indeed work with them. Nasty old girl she is. But she's our only living relation left, so me and Posy have to live with her," was Davy's reply.

"I hope May can keep the necklace safe. If the Lodges got their hands on it..." Jo's voice trailed away desperately. "She will, don't worry. I know her brother; any sister of Mack Rivet can keep their head."

"*Mack*? What's so special about him?" said Jo, frowning. "Fire there was once in the blacksmiths. Cool and calm he was, chucked a bit of water on the fire and saved lots of equipment. That's how he got to be a partner in the business."

"No! Really? He never told *us*," said Jo.

"Can't we just concentrate on escaping?" interrupted Ursula. "How?" said Davy. He tried to open a door. "Locked," he said.

"I wonder if Posy and May are okay," he said after a while.

"They will be probably," said Ursula, "for after all, they don't *know* anything."

"True," said Jo, "but we do, at least, I got stolen because Mr Lodge had a spite against me."

It was at this point that Davy realised

there was a gap between the driver's cab and

the front, almost like a taxi, and that the

drivers could hear everything they were saying.

Were they letting slip information? He felt they

were.

"Hush!" he whispered, pointing to the tiny

hatch.

And so they all fell silent.

Chapter 9: "Beryl!"

Davy, Jo and Ursula were bundled into a cellar together. After an hour, a girl came shyly into it. She wore a ragged dress and held a candle high.

She was short with long fair hair and big green eyes. She softly walked forward, shut the door and said, just loud enough for them to hear:

"Shall I rescue you?"

Jo wasted no words. "Yes," she said at once, "please do! We wish to be rescued and taken to Rose Road at once..." her voice died away.

For the girl, spotting Ursula, exclaimed, "*Ursula*!" in a great tone of surprise. Ursula jumped up and hugged the girl warmly.

"Cousin Cathy!" she said joyfully. "Now

you are here, Cathy, all is sorted!"

"It is," replied Cathy. And she turned to Jo, raised her hands in shock and said in a choked tone, "*Beryl*!"

"How do you know my mother's name?" said Jo angrily. "Because I do," said the girl with a sudden stately dignity.

Jo had never seen her before, but clearly Davy had as he stared at her in shock.

"Beryl was my dog, and she could talk, because Connie let her. My nan took her so she could have some pups, a few years ago. Then she said Beryl had died. I never assumed she hadn't, but I was very upset. Then Connie got stolen, and then I was kidnapped because I was the owner of Connie. I was unhappy. But now I've found you, Ursula, and *you*!" Cathy gestured to Jo.

"I am not Beryl. I am her daughter Jo. My

owner is May Rivet and she helped to gather my mother's pups during wartime; therefore she had a choice of pups and picked me. My mother did die because a bomb hit her," and Jo glared at Cathy.

"I am the Duchess of Northumberland," Cathy replied, "and me and Ursula used to live together. Then because of Connie, some thieves took me...and then Ursula."

"Whom is Connie?" said Davy suddenly. He stood up.

"Connie? Oh, she is my necklace. She has been in the Northumberland family for years; she is a golden necklace with a magic amber pendant and a silver clasp. She was my best friend and advised me on how to look after my estate; however, she got stolen a year ago. I miss her sorely. Anyway — what?" and Cathy gazed across at Jo.

A Tale in Time

Jo stood up. "You'd better hear my story," she said, "because it's of terrible significance to you.

There was a girl called Josephine O'Connor. Davy is her sister. They came from Ireland, but, being orphans, they had to live with their aunt.

When we first met Josephine, my mistress, May, was very kind to her. Josephine gave her a grubby golden necklace. May had it cleaned and realised its true value, then, when she learnt her brother was very ill, she tried to sell it. But it being of a strange useless gold, no one would buy it. Eventually she found money for her brother in a different way, and kept her necklace.

On the second meeting with Josephine, May slipped on a paper package and when she found out what it was, the amber, she clipped it onto the necklace. The necklace thanked her and then became hers.

She wished for me to talk, and then she wished to be on a mountain peak. It was such bad chance that two mountain hikers should have overheard us discussing the necklace's powers, for they recognised it as yours and tried to steal it.

One died, but the other managed to survive and hold onto us as May wished us back in London. Then *I* was stolen. I don't know whether May has the necklace or not, if she is okay or not, and *my* fate is of no matter to you." Jo finished breathlessly.

Davy said sharply, "So you, Duchess Cathy, owned the necklace. It got stolen, the thieves (the Barterhats, the Lodges and my aunt working together) lost it because Josephine stole it, thinking it pretty, and then lost the amber half of it; she gave the chain to May,

A Tale in Time

May found the other half of it and put it

together; two thieves climbing the mountain

she was at the top of heard her talking about it

and tried to steal it; one died, the other

survived and stole Jo; meanwhile, *you* got

kidnapped and then, because you didn't

actually know where the necklace was, Ursula

got kidnapped too. The thieves thought maybe

you stole it back from them; that's why they

kidnapped you. Then me, Jo and Ursula got

taken from the Lodge's cellar to the Barterhat's

cellar, and joined up with you. All this time,

May still has the necklace (probably) and might

try to rescue us."

"She won't need to," said Cathy, smiling.

"I managed to write a letter and throw it out

the coal chute. A return letter has been sent

from the police and they shall come later today

to rescue me. As for you, Davy, and your sister

A Tale in Time

Josephine, you shall both live with me, as will Ursula. I am nineteen, but I love companions. You will be great friends for me and substitute Connie; Jo's owner can keep her."

At that moment, the police flung open the cellar door. Mrs Barterhat, Mrs and Mr Lodge and Davy's aunt stood there handcuffed.

Chapter 10: The Final Moments for the Necklace

May knew of only one thing to do when Davy vanished. She ran for her family.

With a few minutes, May, Josephine and the other Rivets were standing outside Josephine's aunt's house. But they had missed the critical moment; when the prisoners, tied up, were flung into a car and driven away.

"The police," advised Mr Rivet. John turned and ran off quickly to phone them. Mrs Rivet hugged Josephine warmly. "There now, girl, don't worry. Your brother will be found," she said.

Then a loud tannoy announcement sounded:

"Will the Rivet family from Rose Road please report immediately to their house, by

A Tale in Time

Duchess Northumberland's orders!"

And then, a bark, loud and clear, from Jo.

May was off. She ran like the wind down the streets, dodging the cars and flying into her road. Jo was there, and so was Davy, and two other girls she didn't know.

She hugged Jo again and again, and Josephine hugged her brother, and quietly the other two girls stood behind.

Then May glanced up. "Who are you?" she said. The taller older one answered:

"I am the Duchess of Northumberland. My name is Cathy, and I was the old owner of Connie the magic necklace. However, I'd rather you keep her. This is my cousin Ursula, and Josephine and Davy will live with me."

May accepted it all at once. The only thing that mattered was Jo. She would be invited weekly to the estate of Northumberland to see her friends, and she was to keep the necklace.

Suddenly a man came running down the road. In an instant he had knocked May over, grabbed the necklace and taken off.

The police pursued him, Jo and May did, everyone did. But he got away.

"Oh Connie, Connie!" sobbed Cathy a few weeks later when she learnt that the necklace wasn't to be found again. "Ursula, Posy, Davy, I think we'll have an national funeral for Connie, the amber necklace that didn't deserve to be stolen!"

It was so big a funeral. Everyone went, even the Queen.

But only three souls at the front of St Paul's cathedral, where the funeral was held, were silent, grim-faced and bearing it worse then the others.

Jo, poor Jo, with her face woebegone;

after all they had done for the necklace, to

have it taken so quickly, so harshly, by a thief,

it was more then she could bear.

Cathy was feeling dreadful too. If only she

hadn't been so careless with her companion

Connie! She felt remorseful and wished one

day she might hear of Connie again.

And lastly May, who wept unashamedly,

feeling despair. After all, the kidnapping of her

best friend Jo was bad enough. But then to

have the necklace, who befriended her and

helped her get back Jo, stolen the way it was,

just when she thought it would be safe

forever...It felt wrong!

Even the necklace's last deeds had been

good: it had given Cathy and the Rivets piles

of gold and every time one piece was taken

from the pile, it was replaced by another.

As the funeral attendants filed out of the

cathedral's doors, May bent her head and said to Jo, "What an adventure. We shall never have greater."

"No, that we shan't," replied Jo decidedly. "But will the necklace?"

A Million Moments of Adventure

Chapter 1: Peculiar Time

I have been sitting here for an entire minute now, the seconds keep ticking and time goes on. It's strange how sometimes, time is so slow, and you want to scream, to shake your wristwatch, and eat it, you are so frustrated. Yet at other times, I know I feel there isn't enough time for anything. It doesn't seem to be time itself that makes this difference, but it feels as if.

Perhaps it is, and time is spiteful and goes against your wishes always. Or maybe time is a friend of ours, teaching us patience and goodwill. But it's a long process. Or it's us that causes this variation.

Time and human beings are so different, yet I think they might merge into one someday,

because it can't keep going on *forever* — all
things must come to an end. I am writing in
this journal as quickly as I can now, and I note
I wrote at the beginning time is so slow. Yet
it's just before dinner and I am scribbling as
fast as I can, because horrid Miss Anne is so
particular about dinner time.

I am Tessa Roberts. Me, my sister and
brother are all orphans, and our strict old
grandmother sent us off to boarding school.
Poor William, he got sent to a posh school just
like us, but at least me and my sister Alice
have each other. Alice is oldest, and is
fourteen. But she acts as if she's four; she can
melt any strict heart with her faked cuteness.
In reality she's spiteful and cunning. But as
she's the only thing I have left, I can't say too
much bad of her.

All three of us have nicknames: I am Tess,

A Tale in Time

Alice is always known, even by the strictest teachers, as Ali, and William is best known as Will.

Will is youngest. He's eight. But he is clever! He wants to be something good in the world, and I am sure he will be. I'd swap him for Ali in a heartbeat.

There! I did say that all the time I have left now is going to be paining my fingers as I scribble so fast in this little notebook that my words are indescribably messy. If Miss Anne, the elderly, horrid matron of Sally's Seminary, could see my writing, she would give me a lecture on neatness.

The dinner-bell goes now, so I must hide this so my room-mate, Marie, can't see it. She'd only poke and pry, I am sure. I have flown downstairs and gobbled my dinner, chips and pizza, as fast as I could under the watchful eye of that lioness Miss Anne, and then I went

upstairs again.

I had barely settled down to bed when my

best friend, mischievous Louie, had come in.

"So what do you write, Missy Tessa?" she said

in a accurate mimicking of Miss Anne's voice.

"Nothing miss, that I shouldn't," I replied

meekly. She sat down next to me. "Isn't it

horrid being here," she said, suddenly contrite,

"when all other children should be at home

now, with their families, maybe playing a

board game." She peered out the window at all

the cars.

"Hey look, Tess, a sports car in my

favourite colour — dark blue!" she said. I

glanced out. "Oh, that's expensive," I breathed.

"When I'm a rich adult, I'll have one of those,"

she said idly. I watched a man get out of the

sports car. He looked German, with a twirly

moustache. He felt someone looking and glanced up at us. Giggling, we both ducked down and fell onto the bed sideways. "Hey, get off me, Lou," I said, shoving her.

She put her hand to her neck and her fingers fumbled at something. "What's that, Louie?" I said. "What's what?" she said innocently, her eyes suddenly alert as she dropped her hand and pulled her jumper up further about her neck. "It's a necklace!" I cried, spotting sight of it. "Hush, you child!" said Louie frantically as she ripped the thing off her neck. "It *is* a necklace, and if you'll promise to say nothing, I will tell you how I found it." "Yes, do! I'll say nothing!" I promised devoutly.

"I had sneaked out," she announced in a grand whisper. "I went to the library and read a chapter of a book called 'Spotting Magic

Charms'. No sooner had I read this chapter did
I hear the dinner-bell chiming faintly, and I
flew out of the library and crossed the road. On
the other pavement, I fell over — look!" And
she showed a gash on her knee that she had
bandaged with strips of woollen sock. "Oh
Louie! You'd better get it checked!" "And be
put in trouble? I think not!" she said, her eyes
flashing. "Anyway, I had slipped on a brown
paper package and when I opened it, inside
was this." And once more she showed the
necklace. I peered at it interestedly.

It was made of little gold loops attached to
each other, making a chain, while an oval-
shaped amber fell from the middle of it. The
clasp was a polished silver. The thing was old-
fashioned and neat, and when I took it to peer
at it more closely, I felt an almost vibrancy. I
too wanted to chain it about my neck; it gave

a peculiar feeling of joy and delight.

Louie took it back, her eyes shining. "In the book I read, there was an illustration, and I swear, it was the same as this, Tess! I have found a magic charm!" "So the amber is the charm?" I said. Before she could answer, Marie came flying in. "What are you two talking about?" she cried, carelessly banging the door shut. It made a tremendous echoing noise and in an instant Miss Anne's face was at the door, her features full of loathing.

Louie slipped the chain in her pocket, hidden, and sat soberly. "Marie Courser, Louisa Whistle and Tessa Roberts! What is the meaning of this?" said Miss Anne dramatically. "Who slammed that door?" Marie said nothing, her face scarlet with rage. "It was Marie, miss," I obliged. Marie gave me such a look! I nearly burst out laughing. "And Miss Louisa, why are you not in your own room, letter-

writing? To be sure, go there now!" said Miss

Anne wretchedly. "Yes, ma'am! No ma'am!

Nothing of the sort, ma'am!" said Louie under

her breath in a cheeky manner as she slipped

out of the room. I envied her, her room-mate

was Noel Walls, who was a total prankster. I

liked Noel; unfortunately, she didn't like me

because her deadly enemy was Ali.

As soon as Louie had left, Miss Anne did

too, following her, no doubt. Well, Louie lead

her a merry dance! I settled down again, and

Marie came and sat on my bed. "Do you

mind?" I said. "Oh, don't be so particular!

Really, you're as dreadful as Miss Anne! Now,

your sister is a good year older then you, but

she bubbles over with fun from dawn to dusk,

and is as friendly and warm as a baby." "Well,

thank you—" I began coldly. But she laughed. "She'll be coming soon," she said.

Presently I began to write letters to Will, and Grandmother. They must be mundane, praising the school and well written, otherwise Miss Anne makes you write another. Then Ali came in. "Hello Marie!" she said secretively. Then, when I glanced up, she rushed and hugged me impulsively. "How are you, Tess?" she said warmly. But I knew it was all an act, her charming act. "Fine, thanks, you?" I said, those three words as icy as I could make them. "Oh, I'm fine! Now, Marie dear! Have you written your letters? Oh good, you have! For, my dear, I want to challenge you to a good game of Chess." I felt sincerely left out as I finished my, "From your loving sister Tessa—" and folded my letters.

Then I rose and left the room. I walked loudly down the corridor and then tiptoed back and placed my ear against the door. "My sister is early thirteen, but so strange and antisocial," said Ali. I boiled over and rushed down to Louie's room. Noel was just leaving and gave me a queer look, passing by haughtily. I knocked on the door. "Oh Noel, leave me for the moment!" said a voice. "No, it's *me*, Lou, me, Tessa," I said. "Oh Tess, come in — but don't scream or anything!" said Louie. So I entered. "Where are you, Lou?" "Bolt the door first and then sit down," came Louie's voice.

But she was invisible. "Louie? Where on earth *are* you?" "Hush! All shall be revealed in a moment!" came Louie's voice and I did as she said. Then she appeared, laughing breathlessly and holding her necklace. "I have gone," she said mysteriously, "to a world of magic with my little luck charm!"

Chapter 2: "Goodbye, school!"

"You're joking, Louie, I know you are," I said,
but I was nearly convinced. "I am *not*, Tess
dear! I am really not!" Louie threw herself on
the bed beside me, her eyes glowing. "Truly I
am not; I have gone to a magical world and I
want to go again, with *you*, Tess, and never
return!" "Really! But can I return if I want?" I
said. "You *shan't* want to, for it is a thousand
times nicer then where we are now." "Is it then!
I'd go if it weren't for Will. I'd miss him," I said
regretfully. "But we can summon him!" said
Louie, and holding her necklace before her, she
whispered in a low, strange tone, "Let the
magic whirl, till Will is before us!" and then
there was my brother, slightly taller, his mossy
brown hair longer and his face laughing.

"That was a queer experience!" he said,

A Tale in Time

totally believing and not at all shocked. "Was it, Will?" said Louie, at her ease with the stranger. "Whom are you?" he turned on her. She laughed, "I am Louisa," she said, bowing with a teasing properness. "I am pleased to make your acquaintance on a journey which your sister demanded that your presence was with her." "Sister?" he repeated. "Me, Will!" I said. "Oh Tessa!" he said. Too loudly.

Miss Anne rapped at the door. "Children! Open this at once!" "No! Don't!" said Louie, not caring of her voice. "Hold onto me, people!" I grabbed her and Will, and she swung her amber three times around on its chain, and we swirled into the darkness. I felt ground before our feet and we were in a dark hole. "Oh, for the necklace to bring us *here*!" said Louie. "I wished for it to bring us anywhere; anyway, let us sit down and get our breath. Light, please, necklace." The necklace gave off a strange light, and we all sat down.

"What is this, Tess?" said Will. "Louie has come across a magical necklace that will take us or give us anything we want, and we have all left school on a runaway mission." "What about Ali?" said Will unexpectedly. "Oh, her! She was Grandmother's favourite and would only be a pain to us in this journey — don't you think, Louie?" I said. "Who is this Louie?" said Will sharply. "My best friend, Louisa Whistle, aka Louie," I said. "Oh, you own the necklace, do you?" said Will. " "I do indeed," said Louie simply. "Here it is," and she passed it. Will stroked it thoughtfully, and played with it. "Take care not to turn the amber three times around, or something shall happen. That is how I discovered the magic." Will suddenly put it about his neck and did up the clasp.

A Tale in Time

"Whatever are you doing?" said Louie in a voice of shrill suspicion. "Merely seeing how it feels," replied Will thoughtfully. "You're lucky to be able to wear it all the time, Miss Owner." "So I am," she replied.

Will was a tall stout boy of nine with a mossy brown fringe and big clear black — simply *black* — eyes.

Louie was thirteen like me, and had bright green eyes full of a naughty mischief. Her hair was short, shoulder length, and sunny coloured, vibrant, glowing and gold, and her skin was as tanned as a berry. What berries are brown, anyway? As brown as a nut, it would be better to say.

I was dark red, auburn, but my hair fell on longer then Louie's. I used to have a fringe but it exasperated me so I cut it off — most neatly, I think, but Miss Anne scolded me so. My eyes were pure brown, and my skin was pale.

"I am perishing with starvation," said I presently. "Are you! Ah, why did you not tell me, my dear! Will, pass me the necklace. I'll have a royal breakfast for us soon!" said Louie. She turned her amber three times, laughing, and suddenly we were all wrapped up in lovely warm fleeces, far better then our old ones, sitting on the top of a mountain, and with a tray of a hearty meat and bread breakfast each.

Louie and I started devouring, but Will took a mouthful and raised his eyes thoughtfully. "What is this place?" "Only the start of our adventures, my dear boy," replied Louie gravely. "Will we go to this magic world of yours?" said I. "This is the magic world! Oh, absolute freedom! Do you wish to be rich?" "Surely anyone would," I said. "And is there anything you want?" "Why, I'd not mind a little more gravy," said Will. She granted it for him, her eyes glowing with excitement. "We may travel the world, my companions, and have whatever we wish, so long as we have the magic necklace, we are sorted for!"

Chapter 4: The Test of Friendship

"Wish us in Buckingham Palace then," said Will.

Louie shot him a look. "Heh heh, sir, I'm not as foolish as that! Robbers and thieves, that's what we'd be called!" Will leapt at her and snatched the necklace. Turning the amber, he cried, "Let us all be in the palace!" But nothing happened.

Louie, on her back, was indignant and fearful that her charm was broken, and as I helped her sit up, she said, "You burglar boy, pass that to me now! Have you broken it?" "No! Maybe I swung it the wrong way?" said Will worriedly. "No, it works both ways," I intervened. "It does," said Louie, shaking her head furiously. " How could you, Will! Tess, if it is broken, we are stuck on this mountain peak forever!" She turned the amber and a pair of leather shoes came before us. "It only works for its owner then!" she said, relief filling her face. "It seems so," said Will. "So wish us in the palace, please, Louie." "Don't you dare call me by my name!" she shrieked.

Will, bewildered, turned towards me, but I offered no reaction. "Tess, is that the *boy* you have for your brother? A sneaking thing he be!" sung Louie in her rage, and I clenched my fists. "Could you not get on," I pleaded of them. "No! Never!" said Louie in a fine fury; she leapt to her feet, turned her amber, and vanished. "Louie! Louie, you can't leave us!" I said wrathfully.

But she'd just gone and done that. "Now what?" said Will. "Shut up," I said, turning on him coldly. "If it were not for your persistence, Louie wouldn't have left us in such a situation!

A Tale in Time

We may only hope she returns!" I hoped she
would. She was my friend, but Will's enemy.

Will threw himself spread eagle on the
grassy rounded peak and I gazed out and
down, clasping my fingers. Suddenly unable to
stay still, I marched up and down the ridge,
and it was then that I realised the wilderness,
desolate peaks capped with snow, and the way
that this peak was; it was rounded and steep.

We would really starve here if Louie didn't
come back. She would! She must! Even as I
willed these words, she appeared before us,
her arms full of cloth, her green eyes sparkling
and merry, and her hair glimmering in the
sunshine. She threw the clothes down on Will,
making him start up, spluttering in anger.

"There, Mr Roberts," she said joyfully.
"Look, Tess, these are yours." From the bundle
she passed me a gold and black dress, and

then she brought herself a green and red one,

and finally Will sifted through the remaining

articles. It consisted of pink trousers and a

loud yellow jumper which made me glance

away, so painfully bright it was.

We each turned away as one another

dressed, and finally, Will, looking horrified in

his new items, said, "Do you know, Louisa,

that we are stranded here?" "Why call her

Louisa?" I said, holding my hand out to stop

Louie speaking. "Because I should rather be

formal then intimate with her, seeing as I don't

like her," he said simply. "Oh you exasperating

thing, Will," said Louie, "do you want me to

send you back to your school?"

"No! Don't!" he said, horrified. But her

fingers took hold of her amber and sent it

around and around, her mouth formed the

words, and Will vanished. "How could you,

A Tale in Time

Louie!" I said. "He'll be beaten and scolded and punished, whatever you like to call it, he won't get a nice reception back there!" "I have not sent him to his school, but ours," she said, smiling.

There was the touch of cruel spite in my friend. I sighed and shook my head. "Please bring him back, Lou." "I will once we're off this peak; now, do stop badgering me, Tess dear, and tell me where you want to go," was Louie's unsatisfying reply. "I don't know. The world is wide," I said. Louie gave a laugh, "It is," and then stopped and glanced up. Taking my hand, she exclaimed, "What is that?" It was war planes; what was more, they were preparing to shoot at us, thinking us villains.

Louie swung her amber, and we vanished. What a good thing we *did*, for they had nearly shot us. Now we were at a market place, and

A Tale in Time

Louie wished for a discreet purse full of money in her pocket.

We brought meat pastries and asked for lodgings, and were sent to a hotel. Happy in our room, we found out we were at Rome in Italy and rejoiced at our location. "Now," said Louie, locking the door, "shall we summon Will, or leave it a little longer?" I, sitting on the windowsill gazing out at the cars, started and bumped my head.

"*Please*, Louie!" So she summoned him. His face was all red and he shouted, "I won't! Let me go back, let me!" "Hush, hush!" said we both, grabbing him. He flinched away from both of us and said, "I was happy — Grandmother has come for me and Ali — she's going to take us home — let me go back, *please*!" "Why, if you wish!" said Louie, swinging her amber with a recklessness that made my brother vanish.

But his yells had caught the attention of some cleaners and they knocked at the door imperiously. Louie ran over, unlocked the door breathlessly and said, "Forgive me, the noise was from the TV." They, suspicious but believing, went away, and Louie threw herself on the bed with eyes full of mischief. "There, Tess," she said presently, "let us go to the markets."

Chapter 4: Falcon

"For what, Louie?" "Oh, you shall never know what you want till you have seen it. And all the ladies here are so richly decked in jewellery and nice clothes! It would be nice to be as rich as them. Then we shall go to a restaurant and have a gorgeous meal that would make Miss Anne go green with envy!" replied my friend rashly.

I had no disagreements, so we went. Firstly Louie wanted clothes, so we had the loveliest time buying soft heavy material; Louie said that navy blue became her, and insisted on buying a pretty pale green for me, as she said red hair and green goes well together.

We found a little seamstress shop and the young ladies there were going to put our dresses together.

A Tale in Time

I had never seen Louie so merry. Her short sunny hair gleamed rich gold, her eyes were like emeralds and her face was as jolly as it could be. I myself liked this new life of richness, but, I thought to myself, if *I* owned the necklace, I should buy myself a big mansion and live there with plenty of fun features and stay there forever. Louie was restless and I knew she would have to adventure on soon.

We went for a walk up and down the old-fashioned market square; everything was so delightful! And it was when we were chewing on sweet little sugar-covered cakes that Louie darted forward. "Tess," she called, peering over her shoulder at me, "come and see this!" It was a cage; in it was a bird.

He was very big, with beady black eyes, white feathering but a line of black straight across his wings. He had an awesome presence, which made me say, in a scared voice, "Come away, Lou, he looks so big." "Come away? Never! Sir, how much is the bird?" she said to the man in charge of the bird stall. "Ah, madame! I think he is better suited to a hunting lord. A little girl like you should prefer a parrot, yes?" And he showed some docile parrots instead.

But Louie has pluck. Setting her shoulders, she said defiantly, "I should rather have the bird. What is the price?" The price wasn't expensive and she brought him and accepted a leather glove to wear when handling him. "He is a hawk; the best of his type," said the man as he let the bird out of the cage. "Feed him these pellets, madame, and he will stay with you forever and do your bidding." Slipping on the leather glove, so the bird could hop onto her wrist, Louie fed it some pellets.

A Tale in Time

As we walked off, she said lightly, "See how the people stare, Tess! Is it not normal to have a bird on your fist, eh?" "I think not, Lou; it is more accustomed in a grand castle then anything else." Louie shook her head. "A castle is a novel idea, servants and gardeners, a nice retreat from our adventures, set in a lonely mountainside location and with plenty of wooded grounds. It is an idea, Tess, you genius!" And she laughed. "But let us get our clothes and jewellery first," she said.

By now, I had severe doubts of this adventure of ours, and I almost wished to be back at boarding school, where rules were permitted. This sense of glorious freedom intoxicated me, although Louie was doing well with it. She was now on the subject of naming the hawk.

"Let us name it Falcon," she said. "Falcon!

Is that not like naming a guinea pig Rabbit?" I said. "I think it's a good name," she replied obstinately, and she threw her pellets in the air, so with graceful power, Falcon left her, snapped them up and then floated by her. Holding her wrist out, she said, "Falcon!" in a sweet voice and he quickly landed. Louie had a way with her bird; that she admired and respected him was not enough, there was a devout love there too and Falcon returned all three.

After buying some jewellery, we returned to the seamstress's shop to get our clothes, and in an alleyway behind the shop, Louie said, "Let us have a castle full of servants and gardeners, where we need not lack anything, and it must be in a mountainous region, too."

Chapter 5: The Cloud Castle

If only Louie had stayed at The Cloud Castle forever! We were *so* happy there; I, being a more timid character, stayed and explored the clean rooms full of pleasing items; I acquired a dog called Albert, and Albie, as I nicknamed him, was an endearing little thing; scruffy he was and suffered for looks, but was pleasant and loyal to the end.

I did love the gardens too, but there comes the catch, the gardens, full of pretty flowers, not the *grounds*, which were so rugged as to be filled with the wild creatures you will find in the Alps, that being where our modernist heaven was based.

Louie, however, found herself a great black horse called Monster-Breath (as she so charmingly named him) and explored with Falcon the entire grounds, often returning wounded but undaunted. Pluck, that was what she should have been called! She never lacked for spirit, but one day as we sat in our lounging chamber together, she said in a confiding tone, "I wish to leave Cloud Castle and go on in an exploration. Don't you, Tess?" "I have no wish of that," I said grandly, although I knew I would be overruled in the end, and sadly, not gladly.

But Louie put it off, for about a week, and then suddenly she burst into my room at midnight, aroused me, and said brightly, "Come, Tess dear, get warmly wrapped and we'll be off." "No, Louie, I won't go until morning," I said, trying to stand up to her.

But she plagued me and coaxed me and all the while dressed me so rapidly that I was ready in a few minutes and then she took hold

of me and said, "Let us go to the beginning of

all time." And there we were, in the same spot

as where Cloud Castle had stood, but so

strange and desolate!

Everything was different, younger, and

almost uncertain. And I felt dreadfully out of

place in my modern bobble-hat. "Oh, it's *wrong*

to be here, Louie! Go somewhere else!"

Chapter 6: Past, Future, Past

"No, I am enjoying it," said Louie. She didn't look as if she was, but what could I do? — the necklace wouldn't work for *me*.

Now, Louie was an endearing creature, full of bravery and a rash spirit. She never thought twice, and though was not greedy, she was prosperous and desired anything she didn't have; with a necklace that could give her anything, she wanted to make up the most maddest things she could. When she got them, she wasn't happy, but almost irritated.

But Louie was wild, and had an enormous temper that thankfully I hadn't roused yet. I remembered, back at Sally's Seminary, how she grabbed her cousin, annoying Becky Whistle, and shook her by clenching her throat, saying, in a growl, "Don't annoy me, you nosy, hateful *beast*." And Becky never went near her anymore.

Louie also had a touch of cruelty to those that displeased her, and, as she was reckless, this made her do the first thing she thought of, dispatching Will off to *our* school had been cruel, and who knew what she might do to me if I made her angry? I realised that Falcon soared above us in displeasure; Louie had brought him, then! Or, actually, summoned him. Had she truly forgotten him?

I thought of Albie. "Louie?" I said. "What?!" she turned on me with a surprising violence. "Lou, please would you summon Albie?" "If that's all, with pleasure; I thought you'd be annoying me about going back. You are quite untrainable, Tess." I realised Louie had become a spiting thing, even a little detestable, and I wondered with a sigh if she would ever be the old, irrepressible, cheeky Louie of our school.

No, it seemed wealth had ruined her. But I had to check my thoughts as Albie came in my arms and I held him lovingly. "See!" said Louie suddenly, and she pointed, with a tiny stifled laugh, as she made all us invisible, to a massive dinosaur, a Tyrannosaurus Rex, for sure, that strolled along with a comically oblivious nature of our presence.

"Dom Dom!" said Louie. Her voice was audible even if she was not visible and the dinosaur rushed towards us. Louie suddenly vanished. She left me, Albie and yet she took Falcon. "Selfish brute!" I thought as I backed away from the wild beast.

Then I turned and ran. The dinosaur lumbered after me, seeing my prints, smelling

me and hearing me but unable to see me; it
was a clumsy beast but impossibly fast. I
tripped and stumbled, and my hands clutched
upon Albie; suddenly we were both whisked
away and were on a pleasant beach, back in
modern times, and Louie, in the water,
swimming like a goldfish, while Falcon eyed us
all with distaste, called, "I forgot about you!
Sorry!" A maid came on the beach with a
swimsuit and said, "Madame, we are in Spain;
I trust you want swim like other madame?"
"Yes, thanks," I said.

Then I tore into the warm water with Albie;
such a pleasant change to being in the grimy,
damp old times! "Sadia, bring us towels,"
called Louie authoritatively.

As I swam, I gazed about me. The air was
full of things — flying cars! "Are we in the
future, Louie?" "Yes," said my friend

thoughtfully.

As I gazed into the cloudy blue sky, I clenched my fists suddenly. "Where next, Louie?" "I have already decided I want to visit the World War Two's biggest ever fight," she replied nonchalantly.

Chapter 7: The End

"Louie, please don't be foolish," I begged of

her, but it was no use and she persisted in

getting warmly dressed and swinging her

amber.

It was horrible: planes everywhere; bullets

whistling by us but never hitting us. Falcon

was startled; he left his mistress's wrist, and

took off into the air.

Then he plummeted down, shot. "Falcon!

Oh my Falcon!" cried Louie, and she threw

herself forward to catch him. Then suddenly he

was dead, and she was lying on her back,

gasping and struggling with her necklace. "It's

all over for me now, Tess," she said in a thick

blurry voice, and she undid it and handed it to

me. I knew it was mine and she was gifting it

to me, but that was worse then anything else.

A Tale in Time

"Louie! You're only thirteen, you can't die!" I sobbed. "Looks like I can," she said with a carefree smile. Then she was gone. I turned my amber, and said wildly, "Bring Louie back! Oh, let us go back in time to save her!" But I knew it wouldn't work.

The good necklace wasn't going to bring her back. Looking down at the lifeless figure, the green eyes unseeing, the short gold hair never to grow again, her tanned skin to go pale and her bright red lips to never move with lively chatter in this world, I knew I could not be sorrowful and wish her back. Louie the adventurer had gone on to bigger adventures; what they are, I do not know, but she would not have been content in this world.

She asked for an adventure, her little luck charm gave it to her, and now I was to solemnly depart this time and leave her here.

A Tale in Time

Oh time oh time, that one hour ago, she was in the water frolicking like a dolphin with her bird above us; now I sit lonely and deserted in Cloud Castle with my grandmother in her chambers, my brother in an engineering room and my sister trying on her dresses, Albie on my knee, and the necklace about my neck, mine, forever...But even owning the greatest luck charm was not as good as having the humorous brave friendship of Louie...And I leave you now in Time...

I can say I lived contentedly; I cannot say I lived unhappily, but I was never fully at rest because my mind roved, roved like Louie, in that eternity elsewhere, would be...

Tessa

A Tale in Time

Printed in Great Britain
by Amazon

49269886R10058